This book belongs to:

Callie

You are loved

You can do it

Your smile is beautiful

You are special

Being kind is good

Take care of your body and mind

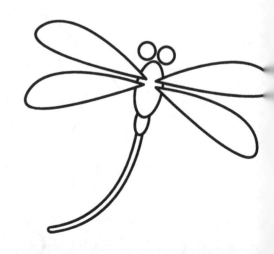

Listen to your parents and teachers

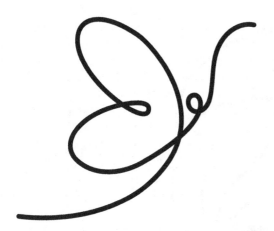

You are a gift

You are brave

Be honest and tell the
tCallie

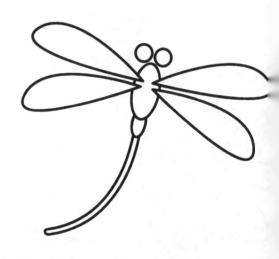

Trying new things is fun

Your ideas matter

You are strong

You are unique

You have a bright future

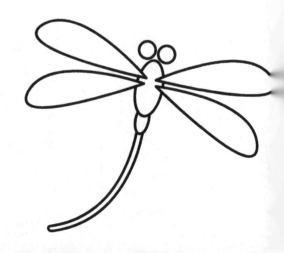

You have a big heart

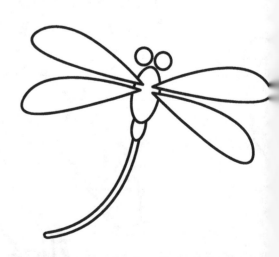

You are helpful

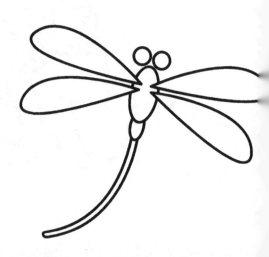

You make the world a
better place

Be a good friend

You are important to others

You are a good Kid

Be a good sharer

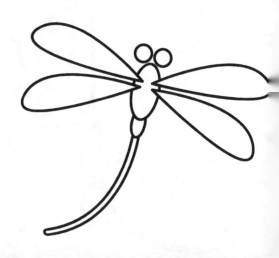

Be kind to everyone

You are full of joy and happiness

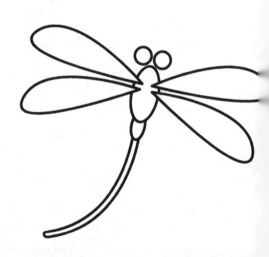

Always do your best

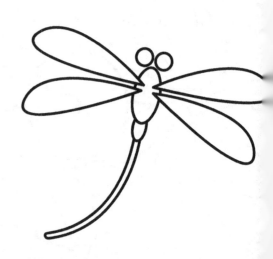

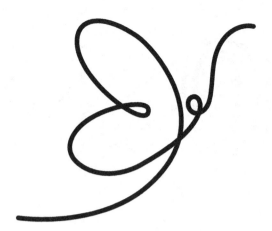

Treat others the way you want to be treated

You are awesome just the way you are!

You have a great
imagination

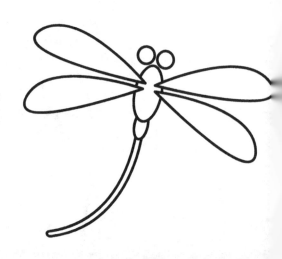

Say please and
thank you

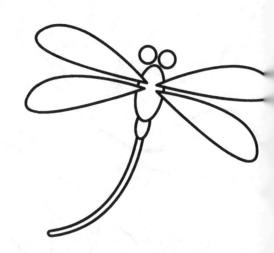

Everything takes practice

It's okay not to be perfect, nobody is!

You are loved by your family and friends

Be grateful for what you have

You can do hard things

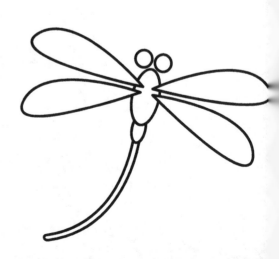

Stay curious

You are smart and clever

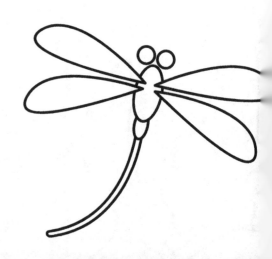

Say 'I love you' to family and friends

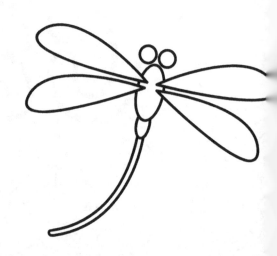

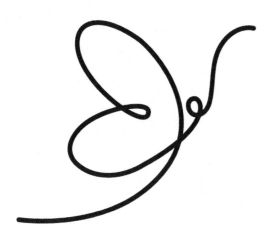

You are important and special

You should be proud of your accomplishments

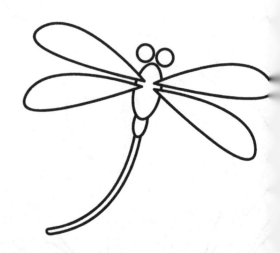

Mistakes help you learn
and grow

You can solve problems

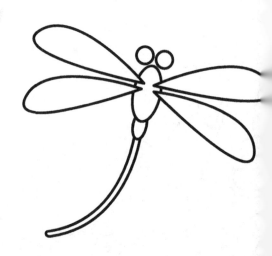

You can do great things

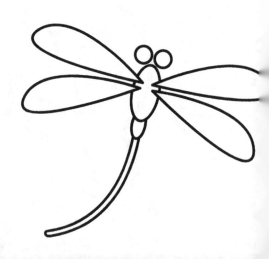

Your brain and body are powerful

You can do anything you set your mind to

If you can't do it the first time, try again!

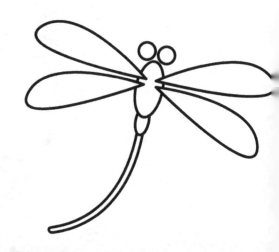

Don't give up, keep trying

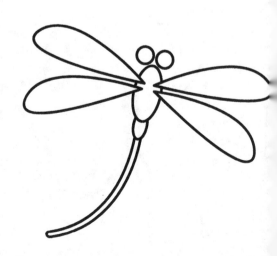

You can ask for help
when you need it

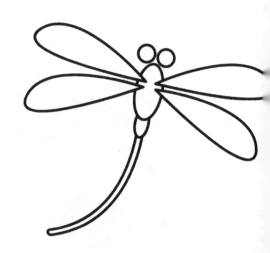

You can make good
choices

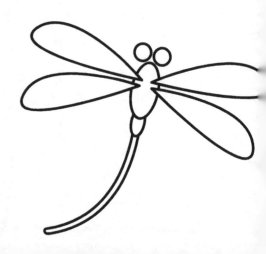

Have a positive attitude

There is no one in the world like you

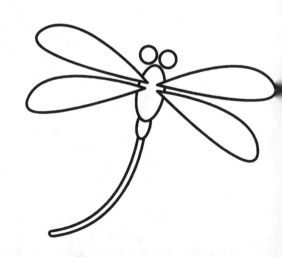

You are talented

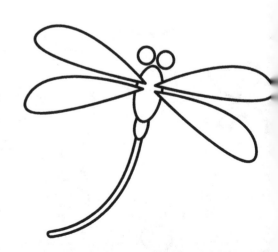

Made in the USA
Columbia, SC
15 December 2023